KU-218-740

Odd One Out

Ian Falk and Bettina Bird
Illustrations by Elisabeth Howell

THE ACADEMY
- 2 MAY 1980
INVERGORDON

Longman Cheshire/Ginn

Longman Cheshire Pty Ltd
346 St Kilda Road
Melbourne, Australia 3004

Associated companies, branches and representatives
throughout the world
Offices in Sydney, Brisbane, Adelaide and Perth
Distributed in the UK by
Ginn and Company Limited, Aylesbury, Bucks

Copyright © Bettina Bird and Ian Falk 1970
ISBN 0 7015 1224 5

First published 1970
Reprinted 1971, 1972, 1973,
1974 (twice), 1976, 1977, 1978

All rights reserved. No part of this publication
may be reproduced, stored in a retrieval system,
or transmitted in any form or by any means,
electronic, mechanical, photocopying, recording,
or otherwise, without the prior permission of
the copyright owner.

Set and designed in Australia
Printed by Commonwealth Printing Press Ltd

To Mrs P. Reilly (Victorian Regional Organiser (Hon) Australian Bird Banding Scheme) and Mr A. West (Director of the Phillip Island Penguin Reserve) for their devoted work with the penguins on Phillip Island from a scientific point of view and in the interest of conservation.

Our thanks for their help with this book.

Odd One Out

Trendset level TS3

1 The Bet

'Today is the start of a whole new life,' I told myself. I picked up my schoolbag and headed for the door. I caught sight of myself in the hall mirror and I giggled. Some people were in for a shock, that was for sure.

'Goodbye, Mum. 'Bye, Dad,' I called out.

'Goodbye, Josephine.' Dad always tried to make me mad by calling me Josephine. Everyone else just called me Jo. That's a good name. I'm really not the 'Josephine' type.

I slammed the front door behind me. Not because Dad made me mad—I'm used to Dad teasing me. It's just that slamming our front door was a kind of game I played with old Mr Trigg. He lived in the house next to us. As soon as Mr Trigg heard our front door slam he'd stare out the window ready to wave to me. We'd played that game for years.

Anyway, poor old Mr Trigg was going to be the first to get a shock that morning. I looked up at his window. He was there all right. I smiled and waved to him. You should have seen him! He didn't even get round to waving back. He just sat there with his mouth wide open, staring at me. You see, I'd had so much of my hair cut off all round since the last time he saw me and that's enough to make anyone look different!

I looked back at Mr Trigg's window before I turned the corner. He had realized by then it was really me—Jo Freeman. He waved like mad.

I was walking across the school yard when Maree caught sight of me. 'Jo!' she screamed, pointing at me. 'What have you done to your hair?' She started laughing. Well, I guess it would have been all right if she had just giggled a bit, but when she doubled right up and had to sit down because she couldn't stop laughing— that was too much! All the kids came crowding around then to see what Maree was carrying on

about. That's when the trouble between Maree and me really started.

I was standing there looking pretty stupid. 'Hey, Jo! Did you have a fight with a lawn-mower?' Nick yelled. 'Hey, Carol, look at that!' He pointed at me.

'Yuk!' Carol screamed. 'Looks like the rough end of a pineapple!'

I can usually stick up for myself pretty well—Carol and Nick knew that—but for once I couldn't think of a thing to say. Maybe that was because I was feeling bad about Max going away so suddenly.

Max was the boy I was keen on. We went around together for ages. He was mad about motor-bikes and so was I. It was really great roaring along on that BSA 650 with Max. I loved the speed and the feel of the wind blowing through my long hair. Then one day Max decided he was sick of school and wanted to look for a job. He just jumped on his BSA and headed for Queensland.

I cried every night for a week after Max left. I really missed him. But you can't go on crying for ever and I got around to thinking that what I needed was a new image—something to help me forget Max. That's why I had my hair cut really short. You see, every time I looked in a mirror, or saw myself in a shop window, or felt the wind blowing through my hair it made me think of Max. Max liked my hair long.

I looked around at all the kids. They were still laughing about my new haircut. Maree was carrying on like some kind of nut, tears rolling down her face. That was when I looked up and saw Johnny staring at me. Johnny was the kid that Maree had been going around with for ages. She was really rapt in him, too. Well, Johnny wasn't carrying on like the others. He wasn't making fun of me at all. When Maree saw Johnny staring at me she stopped laughing and glared at him.

Johnny saw her glaring at him. 'OK, OK,' he said, 'I reckon Jo looks great with her hair cut short.' He sounded as if he meant it, too. You can bet the kids shut up then. Everyone looked at Maree. She was still glaring at Johnny. Then she turned around to me. Her face was bright red. She looked about set to explode.

'Maree . . .' Johnny said. But Maree just turned around quickly and walked straight into school.

'Well really!' Carol said. 'Who'd have thought Maree would go right off like that?' I thought Maree was being pretty silly about the whole thing too. Johnny didn't mean anything when he said he liked my hair short. He just felt sorry for me, I guess. Besides, what did I care about Johnny? He was a nice kid and all that, but next to Max the rest of the gang at school seemed like a lot of little kids.

After school that day we all walked along the street together. Maree made sure she had Johnny right next to her. She wasn't going to let Johnny out of her sight after what had happened that morning. I was walking with Jan and Dean. Jan was telling Dean that she couldn't understand the science homework we had to do that night. Poor old Jan, always worrying about something. Carol and Nick were walking along in front of us. Carol turned round. 'Hey, who's coming to Maree's place?' she called out.

'No need to ask,' Maree said. 'They're all coming. They know I've got some new records.'

'I can't come,' Jan said. 'I've got all that science homework to do.'

'Just listen to her!' Carol said. 'She's beginning to sound like Hal Jones, the way she carries on about her old science.'

You should have seen the look on Jan's face! *'Hal Jones!'* she screamed. We all roared laughing. Poor old Jan. She didn't look a bit happy, and no wonder. Who'd want to be like Hal? Hal never thought of anything but science and maths and stuff like that. At least Jan wasn't that bad yet.

'Here we are,' Maree said. 'I bet mum's got something for us to eat, too—like that chocolate cake Johnny likes.' She smiled at Johnny. Then she grabbed Jan by the arm. 'Come on, Jan,' she said, 'you're coming too.'

Maree's place was great. The gang always ended up there after school. And Maree was right—her mother had made chocolate cake. Carol stood there looking at it. She shook her head. 'Look at that cake!' she said. 'Every bit of it fattening. And I just *know* I'm going to eat at least two bits. Honest, Maree, I'll just have to stop coming round here after school. It's no wonder I'm getting fat with all the things your mum gives us to eat.'

Nick put his arm round her. 'Why worry, kid?' he said. 'No need to start worrying until you hit eighty kilos. You're only seventy now, aren't you?'

'Nick Baxter!' Carol yelled. 'I am not fourteen stone.' Nick grabbed her hand before she could hit him. Carol and Nick were always fooling.

Jan and Dean came in from the kitchen with mugs of hot coffee. 'Coffee!' Jan called out.

I was sitting down eating some cake and drinking my coffee. Carol had stopped fooling with Nick. She was staring at me. 'Hey, Jo,' she said, 'why did you get your hair cut so short?' She sounded as if she really wanted to know. The rest of the kids stopped talking so they could hear what I said.

'I guess I just wanted a new image,' I said. 'After Max and all that. You know what I mean.' That was the real reason, too.

Jan burst out laughing. '*A new image!* Golly! That's a whole new face!' The other kids laughed. It really must have looked funny to them, but I didn't want them laughing at me any more. It gets a bit hard to take after a while.

'OK,' I said. 'It's my new image, and that's that. I like it.'

'That's OK with us,' said Johnny. He grinned at me. 'Isn't it?' he asked the others. All the kids reckoned they liked it too. I smiled at Johnny, not because I meant anything—it was just that Johnny made me feel better.

Maree was very quiet. She was trying to stack up her records. They were all over the room. She kept looking at me, though, and I had the feeling she still had something on her mind. She was standing by the record player with a stack of records in her arms.

'Hey,' she said. 'Talking of Hal Jones . . .'

'Who's talking of Hal Jones?' said Carol. 'We're not.'

'We were before,' Maree said. 'On the way home from school. You remember?'

'So what?'

'Well . . . I've been thinking,' Maree said. She was looking straight at me. Here it comes, I thought. This is what Maree's been stewing over all the time she's been messing around with those records. But I wasn't ready for what Maree said then. 'Jo Freeman,' she said. 'I bet you anything you like you can't get Hal Jones to come to my end-of-term party with you.' All the kids stopped talking. They turned around and stared at her. I stared at her too. I just couldn't believe my ears.

'Big joke!' Carol said. 'Don't take any notice of her, Jo. No one could win a bet like that.'

Jan giggled. 'Well, really . . . Who'd *want* to win it! Carol's a nut if she thinks I'm like Hal. At least I don't *look* like a scientist. *He* does. Those glasses of his take up half his face!'

'And anyway,' Carol said, 'when did Hal ever look at a girl?'

Nick laughed. 'Never, of course! Hal's too interested in frogs and rats and all that sort of scientific stuff.'

But Maree wasn't worried about what the kids said. 'That's what I mean,' she said to Nick.

'Let's see if Jo can get Hal to take some notice of girls for a change. Well it's about time he did, isn't it? I mean he can't spend all his life cutting up frogs and rats!'

'You don't know Hal very well, do you?' Dean said. Everyone laughed. Everyone but Jan, that is. Jan was thinking.

'Come to think of it,' she said. 'Who *would* you go to Maree's party with, Jo? I mean Max isn't here now. He can't take you. And you've got to go with someone, don't you?'

'Yes,' said Maree. 'Why don't you get Hal to come with you, Jo?'

Nick laughed. 'Boy, if you could do that, Jo, you could do anything.'

'Yes,' Carol said. 'Why not? Go on, Jo, have a go.'

'Anyway, Jo,' Dean said, 'Hal's not such a bad kid. It might do him good to get out for a change.'

Maree smiled at me. 'OK, Jo. What about it?'
I knew what Maree was trying to do. She was
trying to get me tied up with Hal Jones just to
make sure I stayed away from her Johnny. I
tried to look as though I couldn't care less.

'You're all crazy,' I said. 'The whole idea's just
one big joke.'

Maree slammed straight back then. 'I *dare* you,'
she said. She was standing right in front of me.
She was holding the stack of records so tightly
her knuckles were white. She looked straight at
me. 'I *dare* you,' she said again.

I didn't take Maree up on that bet. I mean, I
couldn't try to get a kid interested in me just
to win a bet. Maree must have been out of her
mind. And as for me being interested in Hal
Jones—well, that was a laugh! Any boy I fell
for would have to be something like Max. And
I couldn't see Hal roaring down the road on
a BSA 650! Not Hal—he'd die of fright.

But I couldn't get to sleep for ages that night. There was something about Maree and that bet that worried me.

2 Rats and Frogs

Wouldn't you know it! In science the next day we had to cut up a frog. I was in a group with Maree, Carol and Jan. Well, our frog had been stewing in some chemical or other and it smelt like it hadn't been there nearly long enough. Boy, did it stink! Jan had to go out of the room for a while—that was just after we made the first cut down the frog's stomach. Poor old Jan, she was really green. Maree went outside too. She said Jan needed someone to look after her. I grinned to myself. Digging around inside that frog didn't worry me much. I thought it was pretty interesting.

While we were packing our things away Miss MacKay called for some quiet. 'Right, girls and boys, while you are packing up just listen to me carefully, please.' Miss MacKay was pretty young for a teacher. All the boys went right off about her—cleaning blackboards for her and all

that sort of thing. I guess she was OK. She always wore terrific way-out clothes. I liked that.

'Jo Freeman,' Miss MacKay said, 'please don't drop that frog back into the jar from a metre up in the air . . . *Jo Freeman!*'

'Sorry, Miss MacKay,' I said. I didn't tell her that the frog just slipped out of my hand. I hadn't meant to drop it.

'Everyone listening now?' Miss MacKay said. 'Good. Now you all remember what I told you about the penguins down at Phillip Island, don't you? Well, I'm pleased that Hal Jones . . .'

'Good old Hal,' muttered one of the boys.

'Quiet, please! As I was saying, I'm pleased that Hal Jones is helping with the work down there, but more people are needed now, and I would like someone else from this form to come along and help too.' No one made a sound. 'You will find this work interesting,' Miss

MacKay went on. 'Besides it means a day at the beach now and again—right away from the city.' She looked around at all the faces in front of her.

Maree and Jan were back inside now. I could feel Maree looking at me. I knew what she was thinking—she wanted me to put up my hand and say I would like to help with the penguins. Well, Maree could drop dead! I wasn't going to chase Hal Jones just to please her. Maree was standing right beside me. 'Go on!' she whispered. 'What about the bet?' I didn't move. Suddenly Maree pinched me. I let out a yell and swung around. I was really mad. That pinch hurt! My face was red and I knew there were tears in my eyes.

'Jo Freeman!' Miss MacKay said. 'What do you mean by screaming like that?'

All the kids were looking at me. Some of them giggled. 'I'm sorry, Miss MacKay. It's just that . . . well . . .'

Maree butted in. 'I had something to do with Jo yelling out,' she said. She smiled at Miss MacKay. Maree can smile just so sweetly when she wants to. 'I pinched her, Miss MacKay, but I only did it to make her speak up. Jo wants to help with the penguins, Miss MacKay. I know she does, but she won't tell you. I think she must be shy or something.'

Right then I could have murdered Maree!

Miss MacKay looked straight at me. 'Shy!' she said. 'Jo Freeman shy?' The kids all screamed laughing. Everyone was looking at me, even Hal Jones. I bet that was the first time he'd ever turned around to look at a girl. Miss MacKay was looking kind of surprised about the way things were turning out. I mean she'd never have thought of me wanting to help with those penguins. 'Quiet, please,' she said to the form. 'Now, Jo, are you sure you want to help?'

She was waiting for my answer. Everyone else was waiting too. Maree was giggling beside me.

I glared at her. I was trapped and Maree knew it. I had to give in.

'Yes, Miss MacKay,' I said, 'I'll help with the penguins.'

'Thank you, Jo. That's very good of you.'

I went red. Here she was thanking me for something I didn't want to do. I felt awful. I sat down and started packing things into my school-bag. Maree was looking at me, grinning. I turned my back on her. I was never going to speak to Maree again. Never. But Maree didn't seem a bit worried. She picked up her bag and walked out of the room. I bet she was feeling very pleased with herself too.

The other kids had gone and I was left alone. I wondered what Carol and Jan would say to Maree. Maybe they all thought this was just one big joke. Well, it wasn't a joke to me.

None of this would have happened if Max hadn't gone away. Suddenly I felt so lonely I could have cried.

3 Phillip Island

It seemed to take us ages to get to Phillip Island on Saturday. Miss MacKay had told me her car was old and she wasn't kidding. Sometimes I wondered if we'd make it at all.

'Boy!' Hal said. 'One of the shockers must have gone since last Saturday, Miss MacKay.'

'Only one?' Miss MacKay said. She laughed. 'It feels like they're *all* gone!'

I started to giggle. Miss MacKay was different when she wasn't in class. 'Hey,' I said, 'this car makes me think of old Mr Trigg. You'd reckon it would stop dead any time, but it just keeps on going.'

Miss MacKay laughed again. 'I'll tell you what,' she said. 'Mr Trigg must really be in a bad way if my car makes you think of him. Who is he, Jo?'

'He's the old man who lives next door. He's been there as long as I can remember. He lives all alone. I always wave to him when I go out.' I didn't say anything about the game Mr Trigg and I played, because I thought Hal might laugh at me.

'I must look out for him next time I call for you, Jo. I'll wave to him too,' Miss MacKay said. Then she started talking to Hal. 'Have you got that old car working yet, Hal—the one your brother bought?'

That was a surprise, Hal Jones liking cars. I'd never thought of Hal messing around with engines and things. 'Haven't done much work on it yet,' Hal said. 'Haven't had time. But getting that motor to turn over was really something. That motor was a mess, I'm telling you.'

'What kind of car is it?' I asked Hal.

'It's only an old Austin A40, but we think it's great.' He grinned at me.

Then it hit me! Hal Jones—the kid who never took any notice of girls—had spoken to me. In fact he'd grinned at me. Maybe it was because he was away from school that he seemed different. Anyway, I began to realize that I really didn't know anything about Hal Jones at all.

Miss MacKay and Hal talked about cars and things. Then they got around to penguins. I listened but I didn't really understand a lot of the things they were talking about. One thing I learned though. I was one of a bird-banding team. We had to find out all about the penguins at Phillip Island. We were working for some scientists who wanted to make sure the penguins didn't die out. I guess that made me some kind of scientist too. What a joke! Me a scientist! I got a shock when I thought of that.

I got another shock when I learned that the penguins nested in burrows in the sand. That really seemed funny. Who would have thought of birds nesting in burrows? Not me, anyway.

'Better eat your sandwiches,' Miss MacKay said. 'We'll be there soon.' That was OK with me. I was really hungry. I finished my sandwiches just as the car went over the bridge on to the island.

The car stopped at the foot of a hill. There was a kiosk with a big sign in front of it— *Phillip Island Penguin Reserve.* Miss MacKay turned off the engine. Then I heard the roar of the sea, but I couldn't see the water—only sandhills and grass and small bushes. There were no other people around. Even the kiosk was shut and when I got out of the car I felt kind of scared. It was such a lonely place.

'Come on, Jo,' Miss MacKay said. 'Hal, you bring the pack. We've got a lot of work to do before dark.'

I followed Miss MacKay and Hal through a gate in the wire fence that closed in the penguin reserve. Only people with special jobs could go in there. Anyway, that was when I saw the footprints—thousands and thousands of little three-toed tracks all over the sand between the clumps of grass. They looked funny, somehow, all those little tracks, and I started to giggle. 'Hey!' I said. 'Just look at all those footprints! There must be thousands and . . .' I stopped. Hal was grinning at me. Suddenly I felt silly. What an idiot I was to get excited over some-thing like that! After all, Miss MacKay and Hal did this every week. No wonder Hal was grinning at me.

'Jo! Careful where you walk! The penguin burrows are everywhere,' Miss MacKay called out. 'You'll twist your ankle if you're not careful.'

I couldn't see the burrows at first, but they were there all right—just black holes in the ground under clumps of grass. 'But where are the penguins?' I asked. 'I thought there'd be penguins all over the place. I want to see a penguin.'

Well, you should have heard Hal laugh! Miss MacKay just smiled. 'You wait, Jo. By the time you've finished today you'll have seen enough penguins to last you a life-time,' she said.

It was rough going, walking through the penguin reserve. Apart from watching out for burrows there were clumps of grass that got in the way and sand-hills to climb up and down. Boy, was I ready for a rest! 'How far to go now, Miss MacKay?' I asked.

'We're here, Jo. This is our part of the reserve, between these sand-hills. All the burrows here are numbered. See, there's a stick with a number on it beside each burrow. Come on now, let's get started.'

I was thinking that maybe we could all sit down for a while and have a bit of a rest. But no—not a hope! 'Come over here, Jo,' Miss MacKay called out. 'The penguin in this burrow

should still be sitting on its eggs. I'll get it out for you.' Miss MacKay put on a thick glove. She lay down on the ground and put her arm right down the burrow. By that time I was really looking forward to seeing the penguin. I got down on my knees beside Miss MacKay. 'Ah, it's there, all right. I can feel it pecking the glove,' Miss MacKay said. 'There, that's got it!' She pulled the penguin out of its burrow. The penguin wasn't a bit pleased about it,

I'm telling you. Its flippers were going up and down and it kept digging its feet into the sand. It looked really funny and I laughed.

'See the little metal band round its flipper, Jo?' Miss MacKay said. I nodded. 'Every banded penguin has a number. There it is on the band. That's how we tell one penguin from another— by the numbers.' It seemed to me that being a bird-bander had an awful lot to do with numbers and I never was any good at maths.

Then Hal yelled out to me. 'Hey, Jo, come over here.'

'You go and help Hal now, Jo,' Miss MacKay said. 'He's ready to start work.' She put the penguin back into its burrow.

Hal had his back to me when I went over to him. 'Here, hold this for me,' he said. And before I knew what was going on Hal had turned around and put a silly-looking bundle of fluff into my hands.

'Hey, it's alive!' I yelled. Did I get a fright when that bit of fluff started pecking me!

'Of course it's alive,' Hal said, and he started to laugh. 'It's a penguin chick.'

'That was mean, Hal Jones. You might have told me it was alive.'

Hal grinned. 'You would have yelled a lot louder if it had been dead, wouldn't you?'

I guess he was right. Anyway, it was really something to find out that Hal Jones could be funny—if you could call what he did funny. But I didn't have any time to think about it, because right then we started work. One thing I'll give Hal, he really knew what he was doing with those penguins. And that was a lot more than I did. He had that chick in a sack and the sack hanging from a spring balance before I really knew what was going on.

'Hold this,' Hal said, giving the whole lot to me. 'Now read off the weight to me.' He got

ready to write the weight down in a book.

'How do you tell what the weight is?' I said.

'Just look at the pointer,' he yelled at me. 'It's pointing right at the number.'

When I said, 'What pointer?' I thought he'd have a fit. 'Keep your hair on,' I said, 'I'll learn.'

'Yeah,' he said, 'but can we wait that long?'

Anyway, after that things went along pretty well. It was hard work, though, and I soon stopped thinking of those chicks as 'fluffy little bundles,' I can tell you.

It was pretty late when we stopped work. I'd never been so glad to sit down in my life. 'Whew!' I said. 'Thank goodness that's over!'

'Thank goodness *what's* over?' asked Miss MacKay.

'Well, the work *is* over, isn't it?' Suddenly I knew the work wasn't over. I could tell from the look on Miss MacKay's face.

'No, Jo, there's still plenty to be done after dark,' she said. 'But I think you've finished for the day. After all, you've never seen the penguin parade, have you?'

'No. What's the penguin parade?'

'That's when the penguins come back from the sea. They're full of fish to feed their chicks. They look really funny waddling up the beach. Do you want to see them?'

That sounded like a good idea to me. 'Thanks, Miss MacKay,' I said. 'Where do I go?'

'Anywhere along there, Jo,' she said, pointing towards the beach. 'But don't go past the wire fence. It's hard to find your way around here when it gets dark. Have you got a torch?'

'Yes,' I said. 'It's Dad's. It's not very big, but I guess it will do.' I started to walk away.

'Oh, and Jo, don't stay away too long.'

'OK, Miss MacKay.'

I walked past Hal. He was sitting on the ground eating an apple. 'I'm going to watch the penguins come in,' I said.

He waved the apple at me. 'Well, don't get lost. Can't say I'm too keen on the idea of being a one-man search party.'

'Huh! Funny!'

'No joke, I mean it,' he said. 'It gets pretty dark around here. Besides you might fall into a burrow.'

'Yeah, I know—I could twist an ankle or something.'

'Who's worried about your silly ankle! I'm worried about the chicks when you stand on them.' Hal grinned.

I turned my back on him and walked over the sand-hills. I knew he was only trying to make me mad. But just because he knew so darned much about penguins was no reason to pick on me.

4 The Whole Black Night

I sat on a sand-hill overlooking the beach. The sea looked cold and black. The white of the waves made funny patterns on the wet sand. The sky was getting darker and soon I couldn't even see the white on the tops of the waves. I wondered how I was going to see any penguins at all in the dark, but suddenly the beach was lit up. The light was coming from somewhere near the kiosk.

I remembered what Miss MacKay said about not going past the fence, but that seemed silly now. There I was sitting in the dark when I could have been down near the kiosk in the light. I got under the fence, ran down to the beach and started to walk towards the lights. That was when I saw all the people standing around waiting to see the penguins come in. I got a surprise, I can tell you. I hadn't expected to see a crowd like that.

Just as I moved into the crowd the first lot of
penguins tumbled out of the water on to the
beach. They picked themselves up and just
stood there looking at the people and the lights.
Then they turned around and ran straight back
into the water. Everyone around me laughed.
I guess I was laughing too. Everything those
penguins did was funny, even the way they
played 'follow the leader' up the beach. They
were so full of fish they could hardly even
waddle.

And would you believe, those penguins walked right through the crowd! We couldn't move because there were penguins all around our feet. The chicks had come out of their burrows in the sand-hills by this time. The noise those chicks made squawking for food was terrible. Anyway, I was having such fun I forgot all about Hal and Miss MacKay. I didn't think of them until most of the penguins were up in the sand-hills. Most of the people had left by then, and I knew I'd better get back fast or Miss MacKay would murder me. I decided to cut straight through the reserve. I set off into the dark.

It wasn't until I'd got into the sand-hills, away from all the lights, that I realized my torch wasn't nearly bright enough. It only threw a small circle of light in front of my feet. And in all those sand-hills and bushes that bit of light just wasn't enough. I'd never seen a place so dark. It sounds silly, but everything around me seemed the same kind of black. It was all right for the penguins—they could see in the dark. But I was no penguin. I didn't know which I was scared of most—Miss MacKay getting mad with me for being away so long or walking through those sand-hills alone in the dark with all those squawking penguins around me.

Anyway, I had my mind made up for me. By the time I'd tripped over a thousand times and just missed standing on hundreds of chicks, I knew I couldn't go on. I turned around, ready to go back to the kiosk and wait for Miss MacKay by the car. That's when I caught my foot in a burrow and came down hard.

I wasn't hurt. Not really. But when I fell I must have hit the torch on something because the light went out. Everything went black. I couldn't see a thing. I was scared then. Really scared. I sat up and shook the torch. Nothing happened. I turned around to see how far I'd come. Just then all the lights on the beach and at the kiosk went out. The darkness seemed to rush right at me.

Then I really started to panic. What could I do? I couldn't just sit there. But I knew if I tried to move I'd fall over something. In the city there's always a light on somewhere—in a house or in a street. But here there was nothing. Nothing at all. I couldn't even tell the top of the sand-hills from the sky. One seemed just as black as the other. And then I thought of the beach. If I could just make it to the beach it would be easy to get back to the kiosk, even in the dark. I stood up. I could hear the roar of the sea. All I had to do was head straight for it.

And that's when I heard it—that awful wailing scream! It came from the bushes right behind me. No penguin ever made a noise like that! I froze. I couldn't think. That scream seemed to tear right through the whole black night. I couldn't move for a moment. Then I turned and ran—ran like mad. It didn't seem to matter where, just as long as I got away from the thing that screamed.

I don't know how many times I fell over. I know I was crying. Maybe screaming, too. I don't remember. I don't think I really knew what I was doing. Then I saw a light in front of me—a torch light. Someone was calling out.

'Hey, Jo! Is that you, Jo? Are you all right?' Hal! It was Hal's voice!

'Hal!' I screamed. He came towards me and I ran straight into his arms. He held me tightly. I was sobbing and talking all at the same time. Hal was talking too, trying to get me to calm down. I was trying to tell him about the awful scream I'd heard. Just as he was listening to me the scream came again. It ended in a kind of sing-song wail.

'Cats!' Hal said. 'Damned cats!'

Hal was still holding me tightly. I looked up

at him. 'Cats?' I said. 'Do you mean that's all it is—just cats?'

'Not *just* cats,' Hal said. 'Wild cats. And more than one of them if they're making a noise like that. My God, just think what those cats will do to the chicks!'

'But Hal, are you sure it's cats?' I asked him. We were walking towards the kiosk by then.

'Of course it's cats,' Hal said. 'Some stupid people just let their cats run wild. Come on, Jo, we'll have to hurry. Miss MacKay's waiting for us down by the car. She's pretty worried about you.'

Boy, was Miss MacKay mad with me! But it was really because she'd been so worried. 'Really, Jo! If you're going to do this kind of thing you'd better not come again,' she said.

But I wanted to go down to Phillip Island again. I liked Miss MacKay. She wasn't like other teachers. I'd even got to like working with the penguins. And Dean was right. Hal wasn't such a bad kid, after all. I promised Miss MacKay I wouldn't get lost again. I meant it, too. It wasn't until I got home that I realized Hal hadn't laughed at me about getting lost.

Even though Hal didn't laugh at me, you should have seen the other kids at school when I told them about it. Boy, did they carry on! But only Maree asked me how I got on with Hal. Of course she *would* want to know that. Maree was never going to be happy until she had me tied up with someone.

5 The Storm On The Beach

'Josephine! Isn't this something to do with you?'

I was doing my homework when Dad came in with the newspaper. It was Friday night. 'What Dad?'

Dad put the newspaper down in front of me and pointed to the headline. 'There,' he said.

The Penguin Parade Must Go On. I grabbed the

paper. 'High winds and high tides have eaten
into the beach at Phillip Island,' I read. 'The
waves cut into the sand-hills, leaving a one
metre high cliff between the nests and the sea.
The parent birds, filled with fish to feed their
chicks, could not make it up the beach to the
nests. Penguins just aren't made for climbing.
There were some hungry chicks on Phillip
Island last night.'

'Is this about your penguins?' Dad asked me.

'Yes,' I said. Suddenly I felt they were my penguins—mine and Hal's and Miss MacKay's. I looked back at the newspaper. 'Bulldozers have worked on the beach all day moving sand back against the cliffs so that the penguins can climb up to feed the chicks tonight,' I read out loud. 'Oh, Dad, I hope the tide's not high again tonight,' I said.

Dad grinned. 'Well, with a backside like yours you'll make a really good bulldozer!'

'Dad!' I was on my feet glaring at him. He was only trying to be funny, but I wasn't in the mood right then. 'It's all right for you,' I yelled at him, 'you don't care about the penguins. You've never seen them. Well, I have, and I don't want all those chicks to die.'

Boy, did Dad look surprised! 'Hey!' he said. 'Hold on, Jo.' I turned my head away, but Dad pulled me around so that he could see my face. Then he put his arm around me. 'Sorry,

Jo,' he said. 'I didn't realize you were so inter-ested in those penguins. It was Max and motor-bikes last I heard.'

'Max and motor-bikes!' I said. '*Really*, Dad!' He knew as well as I did that Max had gone away.

Poor old Dad. He just shook his head. I can't keep up with all this,' he said. 'Anyway, you'd better go to bed now. You're going to have a lot of work to do down at that island of yours tomorrow.'

The tides *were* high that night—higher than they had ever been before. Miss MacKay and Hal came around to my place early in the morning to see if I could go down right away. I slammed the front door behind me as we went out to the car. 'There's Mr Trigg,' I said to Miss MacKay. 'I bet he's surprised to see me up so early on a Saturday morning.'

We all waved to Mr Trigg—even Hal.

We nearly died when we saw the beach at
Phillip Island. It was a real mess. The tide had
dragged away all the sand that had been pushed
up by the bulldozers the day before. The waves
had cut back into the sand-hills, too. There
was a six-foot drop from the nests to the beach.
No penguin could climb up that! The bulldozers were there again, pushing the sand back
into place. We stood on the beach watching
them. 'They'll never get all the beach fixed up

before dark,' Miss MacKay said. 'I think we'll work on the cliffs in front of our part of the reserve. Come on.'

I worked harder than I had ever worked in my life. To start with we had to dig paths in the sandy cliff-face so that the penguins could get up to their burrows. And that wasn't as easy as it sounds. It took most of the day to get it done. By then I was just about eating sand. There was sand in my hair, down my back, and all over my face. 'Do you know what you look like?' Hal said. He was standing there grinning at me.

'No!' I said. 'What?'

'A cross between a scare-crow and a walking sand-castle.'

'Hal Jones! I'll . . .' I grabbed a handful of wet sand and threw it at him as hard as I could. Of course Hal jumped out of the way.

I hadn't noticed that Miss MacKay was working

right behind him. She was just getting up off her knees when the sand hit her right on the back of the head. She let out a yell and fell flat on her face. Hal and I sort of froze. Miss MacKay sat up, wiping the sand off her face. Then she looked up at us and burst out laughing. Miss MacKay was great.

When we had made enough paths for the penguins to walk up we went back into the sand-hills to weigh the chicks. I pulled the first chick out of its burrow. 'You'd better not go hungry tonight after all the work we've done today,' I said to it. But all the stupid chick did was peck my hand.

Hal grinned at me. 'Anyway, I reckon you did a pretty good job today, Jo,' he said. And for some silly reason I felt pleased.

The Play

'One thing about the play, it means we can all get out together—and at night too!' Maree said. 'And we can all go back to my place afterwards for something to eat.'

Carol giggled, 'I can even put up with watching one of Old Colly's plays for that.' Old Colly is our English teacher. His real name is Mr Collins.

We were standing around our lockers, putting our books away and getting ready to go home. Jan turned round and stared at Carol and Maree. 'Whatever are you two talking about?' she said. 'What play?'

'The one Old Colly says we've all got to go to on Friday night,' Maree said. 'Don't tell me you've forgotten about it already.'

'Forgotten about it! I didn't even know about it!' Jan said. 'I missed English this morning. I was late.'

'Then you'll be glad to know we're all having a night out,' Maree said. 'We're going to a real live play.' The way Maree spoke she sounded just like Old Colly, and the kids giggled.

'And you know what will happen if you don't turn up, Jan,' said Carol. 'Old Colly will have your head on a plate for sure.' That was Mr Collins all right. If he told you to do something, you did it—or else!

We walked out of school together. Nick, Johnny and Dean were waiting for us outside. 'Hey, Jo, are you coming around to Maree's place?' Nick said.

'Yes, come on, Jo,' said Jan. 'You didn't come last time.'

'Sorry,' I said. 'I can't. Mum told me to come straight home. We're going shopping.'

It was a lie, but I couldn't help it. I didn't want to go to Maree's place and I had to find some excuse. It wasn't because I didn't get on well

with the kids or anything like that. It was just
that . . . well, Maree's place didn't seem the same
any more. I was the odd one out now that Max
had gone and Maree never let me forget it.

Well, I could get out of going around to Maree's
place all right, but I didn't have a hope of getting
out of going to the play on Friday. The more I
thought about Friday night the worse I felt. All
the kids would be going together, just like Maree
said. They'd be sitting together too. Maree
would be sitting next to her Johnny, Carol would
be with Nick, and Jan had Dean. But who did I
have ? No one.

I walked straight into my bedroom when I got
home and sat down to think things over. If only
I had someone to go to the play with. But what
boys did I know ? Hal was the only kid I'd got to
know since Max left. Suddenly I wished Hal
would think of asking me to go to the play with
him. After all, we'd been getting on pretty well
at Phillip Island. Sometimes I even felt he liked
having me around. Maybe he just hadn't got

around to asking me. I jumped off the bed and walked over to the mirror. Jo Freeman with her short haircut looked right back at me.

I stood in front of the mirror thinking about Hal. Hal was almost like two different people. Down at the island he was good fun. I liked him. But back at school he was the same old Hal, never even daring to look at a girl. 'The trouble with Hal is that he's shy,' I said out loud. 'Even if he did want to take me to the play he'd be too scared to ask me.' I knew that was right, and I nodded. Jo Freeman in the mirror nodded too. I giggled. Nodding and talking to yourself like that is a pretty crazy way to carry on, I guess. But who else was there to talk to?

'*So why don't I ask Hal?*' I said out loud again. Jo Freeman in the mirror looked as if she thought it might be a good idea. 'After all, Hal has to go to the play too,' I said, 'just like the rest of us. I'm not asking him to take me anywhere special. He won't even have to pay for me.' Jo Freeman in the mirror agreed with every word I said. We smiled at each other. We said, 'Thanks for helping—thanks a lot.' Then I walked back to my bed and sat down.

'Now all I have to do is ask Hal,' I said. And that was when I realized that talking to yourself is no good at all, not when you really need some help. I mean, how does a girl ask a kid to take her out? Boy, did I stew over that one! I just couldn't see myself going up to Hal and saying, 'Hal, how about coming out with me?' I laughed right out loud when I thought of saying that.

But something happened at school the next day that made my mind up for me. I was just getting my maths books out of my locker. I was thinking about the play on Friday night and wishing I could catch a cold or something, so I wouldn't have to go. That was when Maree came up to me. 'Hey, Jo, how are Hal and the penguins and things?' she said. 'Just thought I'd ask.' She giggled a bit.

Maree was up to something, that was for sure.

Probably worrying about her Johnny again. Well, I'd had just about enough of her snooping. I shut my locker door and turned around to face her. 'Hal's OK,' I said, 'and the penguins are fine. But what that's got to do with you, I really don't know.'

Maree tossed her head. 'No need to get nasty,' she said. 'I just wondered, that's all.' She turned round ready to go. Then she looked back at me and smiled that sweet smile of hers. 'By the way I'm having my end-of-term party in two weeks,' she said. 'Don't forget you're bringing Hal.'

I had to say something back to her. I just had to. I didn't even stop to think. 'As a matter of fact Hal's taking me to the play on Friday,' I said, 'so of course he'll be coming to your party.'

Maree stared at me. Then she laughed. 'I'll believe that when I see it,' she said and walked off.

I realized then what I'd done. Now I'd just *have*

to ask Hal to take me to the play. There was no way of getting out of it. I hated Maree.

I hung around the lockers waiting for everyone else to go. I knew Hal stayed at his locker longer than all the others. He always made sure he had the right books. I walked up to him when the others had gone. I was feeling pretty scared, too. My knees felt kind of funny. 'Hal,' I said. My voice sounded shaky.

'Hello,' he said, and he grinned at me.

I tried to smile.

'Hal,' I said. 'Hal, I just wondered. Well . . . we all have to go to this play on Friday. I mean . . . Well, I just thought . . .' Boy, did I feel stupid, mumbling like that. 'Look, Hal, what I mean is, I thought maybe you and I could go to the play together. That is . . .'

Hal messed around with his books. He started to go red. 'Ah . . . Look, Jo. I-I'd like to, but you see . . .'

I knew then that Hal was going to say no. I could feel my face getting red. 'OK,' I said, 'OK. Sorry I asked. Forget it.' I turned around and walked straight down the corridor. My face was burning. I felt so stupid I just wanted to die. 'Oh, Hal,' I thought. 'Hal, how could you? How could you?'

I kept out of Maree's way for the next two days. I even went home every lunch-time. I didn't know if Maree had told Carol and the others that I was going to the play with Hal, but I thought she might have. So I stayed away from them too. Those two days were awful. I was so lonely.

One thing though, I didn't have to worry about keeping out of Hal's way. He never came near me at school anyway, and I made sure I sat right in the front of the class. I didn't even have to look at him then. But what hurt most was thinking about Phillip Island. I really liked being there with Hal. I thought he liked me being there too. Now it looked as if he really couldn't have cared less. I just couldn't see how I could ever go to Phillip Island and help with the penguins again.

By Friday night I was really in a stew. I didn't know how I was going to face Maree when I got to the theatre. I'd be the odd one out again, and Maree wouldn't let that go by without saying something. And then there was Hal. He'd be there too—probably standing around talking to some of the boys. I just didn't know how I was going to face Hal.

I got around to thinking that I'd tell Mum I was sick so I could stay home, but it's pretty hard to fool my Mum. I'd just about decided to walk straight into the theatre with my nose in the air when I had an idea. If I got to the play late and left just before the lights came on I wouldn't have to face anyone.

All the kids had gone in when I got to the theatre, but Mr Collins was waiting outside. 'About time, Jo,' he said. 'You're the last.

Everyone's here now except Hal Jones. And he isn't coming, I know that. Pretty good really, only having one of you miss out on this play.'

I followed Mr Collins into the theatre in a daze. Hal wasn't coming. Why? What was his excuse? It must have been a good one or Mr Collins would have been mad.

I don't really remember much about that play. I kept thinking about Hal. I couldn't forget how he'd looked when I asked him to come to the play with me. He had tried to tell me something that day in the corridor and I hadn't let him. I'd just walked off and left him. Maybe he really had wanted to take me but he just couldn't go. Maybe that was what he'd been trying to say?

7 The Blow-Hole

On the way down to Phillip Island the next day Hal hardly even looked at me. I just sat in the car and listened, while he talked to Miss MacKay about the things we had to do that day. It turned out that Miss MacKay was going to drop us off near the blow-hole. The blow-hole is a kind of opening in the rocks. The sea rushes into it and the spray goes right up in the air. Miss MacKay wanted us to walk back along the beach to the kiosk to see if we could find any dead penguins on the way. That part was all right. It was just that Hal and I were going to be alone together, and it was the first time I'd seen him since I made such a fool of myself by asking him to go to the play.

When Miss MacKay drove off Hal started to walk down the hill. 'Come on,' he said. 'Guess you'll want to see the blow-hole.' He hardly even turned his head. He just went on walking.

I couldn't keep up with him he was walking
so fast. I'd never seen Hal in that kind of mood
before. I watched him walk over the rocks.
'This must be the blow-hole,' he yelled. He
turned around to me. 'Doesn't look much,
does it?'

The sea came rushing into the blow-hole behind Hal. White spray shot right up in the air. I could see what was going to happen. 'Hal!' I yelled. 'Look out!'

Hal turned around just as the spray was coming down on top of him. He tried to run but he slipped and fell. 'Hal—Hal, are you all right?' I yelled. I couldn't get across those rocks fast enough.

Hal stood up. He was squeezing the water out of his jacket. 'Of course I'm all right,' he shouted at me. But he looked so funny with his hair all wet and the water running down his face that I couldn't help laughing. 'What's so funny?' he yelled.

'You should see yourself!' I said. I still couldn't stop laughing.

Hal took off his glasses and wiped them. He looked down at his wet clothes. Then he looked up at me and started to grin. 'Rotton blow-hole!'

he said. He grabbed my hand. 'Come on, let's get out of here before it happens again.'

Hal was still holding my hand when we got to the sand. 'Jo,' he said, turning to me. 'Why did you walk off the other day without letting me talk to you? I was only trying to tell you that I couldn't take you to the play.'

We were standing still now looking at each other. 'I thought you were going to say no, Hal. I thought you didn't want to take me.'

'But Jo, I was only trying to tell you that my sister was getting married so I had to go to the stupid wedding. Tell you what, Jo,' Hal said, putting his arm around me, 'I did want to take you. You're the first girl I've ever wanted to take out.' Suddenly I felt happy. Now everything was all right between Hal and me. 'Hey!' Hal said, 'Miss MacKay will be waiting for us. Come on, we've got to see if there are any dead penguins on the beach.'

We walked along the wet sand right down near the water. We had our arms around each other and I was resting my head on Hal's shoulder. 'Hey, there's a penguin,' Hal said. 'Dead, too.' I picked up the penguin. It was one of our banded ones. Hal took the little metal band off it's flipper. 'Better get this back to Miss MacKay,' he said. 'She'll want to look the number up in the books to find out how old the penguin was and everything.'

'Wait a moment, Hal. I want to ask you something,' I said. 'It's about Maree's end-of-term party. Would you like to come, Hal?'

Hal grinned. 'Thanks,' he said. 'I sure won't say no to that one.'

8 . . . and the room spun

I was still putting on my make-up when I heard someone at the front door. 'Josephine!' Dad called out. 'You can't stand in front of the mirror all day. Hal's here.'

'OK, Dad, I'm nearly ready.'

It was the night Hal was taking me to Maree's end-of-term party. We had to be around at her place by half-past five—Maree's mother was turning on all sorts of things for us to eat. I was looking forward to that party.

I took a last look in the mirror and suddenly I realized how much I'd changed since I met Hal. It wasn't anything to do with my short hair. Everything about me seemed different— even the way I felt. All that stuff about a 'new image' seemed a long time ago now.

When I came out of my room Hal was waiting

for me. He seemed about as jumpy as I was, but I knew from the way he looked at me that he liked me.

Hal and I went outside and I slammed the front door hard. I had my hand up, all set to wave to Mr Trigg, but there was no one at the window.

'Hey, just a moment, Hal,' I said.

'What?'

I was still looking up at the window. It was the only time I could ever remember Mr Trigg not being there when I slammed the door. 'Mr Trigg's not at his window,' I said.

'Maybe he's just resting or something,' Hal said. He walked on. 'Come on, Jo, we'll be late.'

But I couldn't go on. I don't know why. 'Hal, don't go away. Something's wrong—I just know it.'

Hal turned around. 'OK,' he said and walked back to me.

I grabbed Hal's arm. 'Look, Hal, Mr Trigg's still not there. I can't understand it. There's something funny going on. I know there is. I'm going to get Dad.' I left Hal standing there and raced inside.

Dad knew about the game Mr Trigg and I always played. Besides anyone could see how worried I was. Dad got out of his chair and picked up the newspaper. 'All right, Jo, all right,' he said. 'I'll come and see Mr Trigg. I have to take the newspaper in to him anyway. I bet he's only out in the kitchen.'

Hal and I followed Dad up to Mr Trigg's front door. Dad knocked but no one came. 'That's funny,' Dad said. 'Never known the old boy to take this long before.' He tried the door. It opened. Mr Trigg never locked his door in the daytime. 'Think I'll take a look around,' Dad said. He went inside. 'Mr Trigg,' Dad called out. 'Are you there, Mr Trigg?' No one answered. Dad walked down the passage. The only sound in the whole house was the sound of Dad's footsteps. Suddenly even that stopped. I moved closer to Hal. He put his arm round me. Dad slowly opened the door at the other end of the passage. 'Mr Trigg . . . Mr Trigg,' Dad said quietly, but nobody answered him. Then I heard the footsteps again. They were quicker now, and getting louder as Dad came back to the front door.

When he came outside again his face was white. He wasn't looking at Hal and me—he was staring out into the street. 'Dad!' I said, 'Dad! What's wrong?' He didn't answer me. He just kept staring. I grabbed hold of Dad. 'Dad! What is it? Tell me, Dad. Is something the matter with Mr Trigg, Dad?' I was shaking him, trying to make him answer me.

Dad looked down at me then. His eyes looked funny somehow—sort of dazed. 'Yes,' he said, 'there is something the matter with Mr Trigg.' Dad put his hand on my shoulder. 'He's dead, Jo. Mr Trigg is dead.'

'*Dead*!' I couldn't believe it. Not Mr Trigg who waved to me every day—who couldn't believe his eyes when I had my hair cut short. Not dead. Not Mr Trigg. I felt cold all over and I wanted to cry, but somehow the tears just wouldn't come. I think I must have been too stunned to cry.

I felt Dad's hand tighten on my shoulder. 'Come on, Jo,' he said. 'Old people can't live for ever, you know.'

'Oh, Dad, Dad!' I said. I clung to him and buried my face in his shoulder. I wanted to cry and cry but the tears still wouldn't come.

Dad was talking to me, trying to make me feel better. 'I want you to do something for me, Jo,' he said. 'I want you to go to the party with Hal.' Dad looked at Hal. 'You'll see Jo's all right, won't you, Hal?' Hal nodded. Hal was looking a bit stunned too.

'But Dad . . . I can't go. I just can't,' I said.

'Come on, Jo, be a good girl. There are things I have to do now, and you'll be better away from the place,' Dad said. 'This is your way of helping. Off you go, now.' Dad waited while Hal and I walked away down the street.

'Come on, Jo,' Hal said, 'your Dad's right. Let's just do what he says.'

I didn't feel a bit like going to the party now, but I guess Dad was right. I'd only be in the way at home. Besides I didn't want to mess things up for Hal. After all I couldn't expect him to feel the same way about Mr Trigg as I did. I'd just have to try to forget what had happened. I mean you can't go through a party in a complete daze, and that's how I was right then—in a complete daze. I'd just have to try to look as if I were having a good time.

Maree met us at the door. 'Come on in,' she said, 'everyone's here. I thought you were never going to make it.' Maree's record player really made that room jump. All the kids were dancing or standing around talking. I was still in a daze, but the noise and the records and seeing all the kids having fun made me feel a bit better.

'Hi!' Carol yelled from the other side of the room. She grabbed Nick's arm and dragged him across the room to talk to us.

Jan and Dean were dancing. 'Hey, where did you and Hal get to?' Jan called out. 'Maree didn't think you'd make it.'

'Don't be silly, Jan,' Maree said. 'I knew they'd come sometime.' She smiled at Hal and me. 'Anyway, I'll get you both something to eat.'

I tried to dance and laugh and talk to people, but I guess I didn't make such a good job of it. All the time it felt as if it were someone else laughing and carrying on—it wasn't really me at all. I don't think anyone noticed, though—except maybe Hal. He looked at me sometimes as if he knew why I was carrying on like that—

as if he knew I was covering up my feelings about Mr Trigg.

'Let's have that record again!' Dean called out.

'Yeah, it's great!'

'Terrific!'

All the kids wanted to hear the record again. 'OK, OK!' Nick said, waving his arms around to shut everyone up. 'Coming right up.'

Hal and I danced together. Hal really wasn't that good at dancing, but he sure had a great time trying. He was really sorry when the record stopped.

Nick was going through the stack of records looking for another one to play. He looked up and saw us standing near him. 'Hey, Hal,' he said, 'I wanted to ask you about that old car of yours.'

'Yeah?' Hal said. He was still puffed from dancing. 'What about it?'

Nick grinned. 'Well, my dad wants to get hold of one like it. He wants to know where you got that one.'

Hal and I walked over to Nick. 'My brother got that car from a mate of his,' Hal said, 'but there's a car yard around in James Street . . .' Hal turned and looked at me. 'Hey, Jo, you don't mind us talking about cars and things for a bit, do you?'

'No, Hal,' I said. 'You two go right ahead. I've got a bit of a headache. I think I'll go and see if Maree's mum can give me something to get rid of it.'

I was on my way over to the kitchen door when Johnny called out, 'Hey, Jo!' I turned around. Johnny came up to me. 'What's the matter?' he asked me. 'You look like your best friend just dropped dead.' For a moment I thought Johnny knew about Mr Trigg, but he wouldn't have said a thing like that if he'd really known. He was only fooling. I tried to smile—tried to think of something to say, but I guess I just stood there looking pretty stupid.

'What's up, Jo?' Johnny said. 'What did I say?'

'Nothing, Johnny. Nothing really.'

'Go on, something's wrong. I can tell by the long look on your face. Is it something to do with Hal, Jo?'

'No, nothing like that.' I didn't want to tell Johnny about Mr Trigg, but I could see I would have to. Johnny wasn't going to stop until he knew what was the matter with me. 'It's just that . . . well . . . something happened before we came to the party. Something awful.' Johnny could see I was really upset about it and he came closer to me. 'What happened, Jo?'

'Mr Trigg died, 'I said. 'He was the old man who lived next door to us. I used to see him every day. He waved to me every morning. And Mum used to cook things for him to eat. I liked old Mr Trigg, I really did.'

Johnny must have seen the tears come into my eyes. 'Gee, Jo, what an idiot I am,' he said. 'Hell, I'm sorry I said anything about dropping dead. I didn't know, Jo.' He put both his arms around me. 'Poor old girl,' he said. 'you've had a tough time tonight, haven't you? But there's nothing you can do now. It's not the end of the world, you know.'

'It *is* for Mr Trigg,' I said. 'You don't understand. Mr Trigg's dead, Johnny. Dead!'

There was one of those funny silences in the room. The record had stopped and everyone was just standing around. Suddenly I saw Maree. She was holding a plate. I didn't know how long she'd been there, but she saw Johnny with his arms around me. I knew that was enough to set her off.

'*Dead*!' Maree said. Everyone in the room heard her. 'Did you say *dead*? I'll tell *you* something. The only thing that's dead around here is Hal Jones. Look at him! I'll bet he's talking about

his old frogs and rats again. If only he cared about girls as much as them.'

My head was swimming. I just couldn't believe this was happening to me.

'And you, Jo, Freeman! You won your bet, didn't you? You got Hal Jones to come to this party and that's all *you* cared about. As soon as you won the bet you dropped him. And now look at you—after Johnny again! I know *your* type.'

Not one person in that room moved. No one. No one—except Hal. Hal walked straight out of the room and slammed the door behind him. He was gone—gone for ever, all because of stupid Maree. I started screaming at Maree. I don't know what I said, because the whole room started turning around me and my legs felt shaky. I went cold all over and my face started to prickle. I was still yelling. I could hear the door slam behind Hal. I could see Mr Trigg sitting at his window—waving to me.

I could hear Maree screaming at me, and the room spun faster and faster. Then I passed out.

.   .   .

I felt really bad the weekend after the party. I wasn't any too happy when Max went away, but that was nothing to how I felt about losing Hal. Carol and Nick made sure I got home all right that night. There wasn't really much wrong with me—it was just that everything seemed to happen at once. Anyway, by the time Monday came I knew I couldn't turn up at school when Hal was going to be there. I just couldn't face him after what Maree had done.

On Monday night I just lay on my bed and thought about Hal. I knew I'd have to go to school sometime—probably the next day, but somehow I couldn't face up to the thought of seeing Hal again.

'Jo!' It was Dad calling. I'd probably only forgotten to wash up or something. Mum and Dad knew what had happened with Hal and they kept trying to find things for me to do. 'Just to take your mind off things,' so Mum said, as if anything could make me forget a thing like that.

'Jo!' Dad called again. 'Will you come out here when I call you, please!'

'OK, OK, I'm coming.' I rolled off the bed and stood up. I was about to go out the door when I saw myself in the mirror. There were red rings around my eyes. My hair was nearly standing on end. I looked a different person from the one I saw in the mirror the night of the party.

'Jo! Do I have to come in there and drag you out?'

Damn the washing up. I wished Mum and Dad would stop thinking of things for me to do. Whatever I did I would think of Hal. Nothing could stop me thinking of him. I went out of my room. 'OK, Dad. What do you want?' I said.

Dad was standing in the passage. Hal was beside him. First I looked at Dad, then back at Hal—just to make sure my eyes were all right. Suddenly I felt as if I was going to pass out again. But Dad came over to me and put his hand on my shoulder. 'Well,' he said, 'I think I'll just leave you two to sort things out.' Dad walked off.

Hal and I just stood and looked at each other. 'Hal,' I started to say, 'I—I didn't know . . .'

Hal handed me a bit of paper. 'Read it, Jo,' he said. 'Tell me if it's true.'

I took the paper. It was a letter. I started reading it. 'Dear Hal,' it said, 'I'm writing this letter to tell you I'm sorry. It wasn't true what I said about Jo and you and the bet. It was really me who made that bet, not Jo. I just got mad about Jo and Johnny, I guess. And I was wrong about that too. Anyway, after you left Jo started screaming at me. She said she really liked you and that I'd messed it all up. She said she'd

never see you again now because of me and I started it all. I guess I did, too. Then Jo passed out and Carol and Nick had to take her home. I know now that Jo really likes you, and I'm sorry about what I did. I just thought you should know how it really was. From Maree.'

I looked up at Hal. He was biting his lip. 'Is it true, Jo? Is it?' he said quietly. His voice was shaky.

I reached out and held his hand. 'Yes,' I said. 'Yes, Hal, it's all true.'

Hal held my hand hard. 'I knew it was!' he said. 'But I couldn't go to school today. I knew I'd see you and I was scared that . . .'

'But I didn't go today because of you!' I said.

I could see the tears come into Hal's eyes and I knew I was crying too, but for some silly reason we both started to laugh together.

And half-laughing, half-crying Hal pulled me into his arms.